Kneller's Happy Campers

Kneller's Happy Campers

Etgar Keret

Translated from the Hebrew
by Miriam Shlesinger

Chatto & Windus
LONDON

Published by Chatto & Windus 2009

First published in Hebrew by Keter and Zmora Bitan in 1998
First published in English in the United States of America by St Martin's Press in 2001

21

First published in Great Britain in 2009 by
Chatto & Windus
Random House, 20 Vauxhall Bridge Road,
London SW1V 2SA
www.rbooks.co.uk

Addresses for companies within The Random House Group Limited can be found at:
www.randomhouse.co.uk/offices.htm

The Random House Group Limited Reg. No. 954009

A CIP catalogue record for this book
is available from the British Library

ISBN 9780701184315

Penguin Random House is committed to a sustainable future for
our business, our readers and our planet. This book is made from
Forest Stewardship Council® certified paper.

Typeset in Baskerville by Palimpsest Book Production Limited,
Grangemouth, Stirlingshire

Printed and bound in Great Britain by Clays Ltd, Elcograf S.p.A.

To Eyal and Shlomo

KNELLER'S HAPPY CAMPERS

I think she cried at my funeral. It's not that I'm conceited or anything, but I'm pretty sure. Sometimes I can actually picture her talking about me to some guy she feels close to. Talking about me dying. About how they lowered me into the grave, kind of shrivelled up and pitiful, like an old chocolate bar. About how we never really got a chance. And afterwards the guy fucks her, a fuck that's all about making her feel better.

chapter one

in which Mordy finds a job and a hard-core bar

Two days after I killed myself I found a job here at some pizza place. It's called Kamikaze, and it's part of a chain. My shift manager was really cool and helped me find somewhere to live, with this German guy who works at Kamikaze too. The job's no big deal, but it'll do for a while. And this place – I don't know – whenever they used to sound off about life after death and go through the whole is-there-isn't-there routine, I never thought about it one way or the other. But I'll tell you this much: even when I thought there was, I'd always imagine these beeping sounds, like a fuzz-buster, and people floating around in space and stuff. But now that I'm here, I don't know, mostly it reminds me of Tel Aviv. My roommate, the German, says this place could just as well be Frankfurt. I guess Frankfurt's a dump, too. By the time it got dark, I'd found a bar – an OK place called Stiff Drinks. The music wasn't bad, either – not exactly up to date, but with character and lots of girls chilling on their own. On some of them you could tell straight off how they did it, with the scars on their wrists and everything, but there were some that looked really good. One of them – definitely hot – came on to me right on the first night. Her skin was, like, kinda loose, kinda droopy. Like someone who'd done it drowning, but she had a bod to die for, and her eyes were something else. I didn't make a move, though. Kept telling myself it was because of Desiree. 'Cause dying and everything just made me love her more. But who knows, maybe I'm just repressed.

chapter two

in which Mordy meets a real friend and loses a game of pool

I met Uzi Gelfand at Stiff Drinks, almost by accident. He seemed really friendly. Bought me a beer and everything, which freaked me out 'cause I thought he must be trying to stick it to me or something. But pretty soon I saw he wasn't on to me at all, just bored. He was a few years older than me and going bald, so the little scar – the one on his right temple where the bullet went in – stuck out even more, and so did the other one, which was much bigger, on the left side, where it went out.

'Used a dumdum,' Gelfand goes, and winks at two girls standing at the bar right next to us, drinking Diet Coke. 'I mean if you're gonna do it, do it right.'

It wasn't until after those two ditched us for some blond guy with a ponytail that he admitted he'd only chatted to me 'cause he thought we were together.

'Not that it makes any difference,' he says, and head-butts the bar – but not very hard, just trying to chill – 'even if you'd introduced me they'd have gone off with some blond guy in the end. That's just how it is. Every girl I meet – they always have a blond guy waiting for them somewhere. But I'm not bitter. No way. A little desperate, maybe, but not bitter.'

Four beers later we were shooting pool, and Uzi started telling me about himself. Turned out he was living not far away from my place, but with his parents, which was pretty weird. I mean most people live alone here, or with a girlfriend maybe, or a roommate. Uzi's parents had committed suicide five years before him. His mother had some disease and his father didn't want to go on without her. His little brother was also living with them. Just got here. Shot himself too, in the middle of basic training.

'Maybe I shouldn't say this,' Uzi smiled and potted the eight ball right into the left pocket, on a fluke, 'but when he got here we were really happy. You shoulda seen my dad, a guy who wouldn't bat an eye if you dropped a ten-pound sledgehammer on his foot. Grabbed him and cried like a baby, no shit.'

chapter three

in which Kurt starts bitching and Mordy's had enough

Ever since I met Uzi we hit the bars every night. There's only, like, three of them here and we hit all three each time just to be sure we don't miss out on any action. We always wind up at Stiff Drinks. It's the best one, and it stays open latest, too. Last night was awful. Uzi brought this friend of his, Kurt. Thinks the guy's really cool 'cause he was the leader of some famous band and everything. But the truth is he's a big-time prick. I mean, I'm not exactly sold on the place either, but this guy, he wouldn't stop bitching. And once he gets going – forget it. He'll dig into you like a bloody bat. Anything that comes up always reminds him of some song he wrote, and he's got to recite it for you so you can tell him how cool the lyrics are. Sometimes he'll even ask the bartender to play one of his tracks and you just wanna dig yourself a hole in the ground. It isn't just me. Everybody hates him, except Uzi. I think there's this thing that after you off yourself, with the way it hurts and everything – and it hurts like hell – the last thing you give a shit about is somebody with nothing on his mind except singing about how unhappy he is. I mean if you gave a flyin' fuck about stuff like that you'd still be alive, with a depressing poster of Nick Cave over your bed, instead of winding up here. But the truth is that it isn't only him. Yesterday I was just feeling crap. The job at the pizza place and pissing the night away at the bars, it was all getting pretty tired. Seeing the same people with their flat Coke every night, and even when they'd look you straight in the eye you'd feel like they were just kinda staring. I don't know, maybe I'm too uptight, but when you look at them, even when you feel the vibes in the air like something's really happening, and they're dancing, or making out or having some laughs with you, somehow there's always this thing about them, like it's never a big deal, like nothing really matters.

chapter four

Dinner at the Gelfands'

On Friday Uzi invited me over to his parents' place for dinner.

'Eight o'clock sharp,' he said, 'and don't be late. We're having bean and potato *cholent* with *kishke*.' You could tell the Gelfands were from Eastern Europe. The furniture was a DIY job that Uzi's father had put together, and they had these god-awful stucco walls. I didn't really wanna go. Parents always think I'm a bad influence. I don't know why. Take the first time I had dinner at Desiree's house. Her father kept looking me over, like I was some punk trying to get a driver's licence and he was the guy from the DVLA who wasn't going to let me pass. By the time we got to dessert, he was hassling me – but trying to make like it was no big deal – to see if I was into getting his daughter to do drugs.

'I know how it goes,' he said, giving me that undercover cop look – the kind they give just before they cuff you. 'I used to be young too, you know. You go to a party, dance a little, things get heated up, and next thing you know you're in some room together, and you're getting her to take a kote.'

'A toke,' I tried to tell him.

'Whatever. Listen, Mordy, I may seem naive, but I know the routine.'

I got lucky with the Gelfands, though, 'cause those kids were so far gone that their parents had nothing left to worry about. They were really happy to have me there and kept trying to stuff me with food. There's something nice about home cooking. I mean it's hard to explain, but there's something special about it, a feeling. As if your stomach can figure out that it's food you didn't have to pay for, that someone actually made it out of love. And after all those pizza places and Chinese takeaways and junk food that my stomach's taken in since I got here, it appreciated the gesture. To thank me, it sent these heat waves up to my chest every once in a while.

'She's a real shark, our mum,' Uzi went, and he hugged his tiny mother really tight without even letting go of the silverware. Uzi's mom laughed and asked if we wanted some more *kishke*, his father got in another lame joke, and for a second there I actually started missing my own parents, even though before I offed myself their nagging used to drive me mad.

chapter five

in which Mordy and Gelfand's little brother do the dishes

After dinner I sat in the living room with the rest of them. Uzi's dad turned on the TV. There was this boring chat show on, and he kept swearing at everyone on the show. Uzi'd had a whole bottle of wine with his dinner and just passed out on the sofa. It was getting pretty tired, so me and Uzi's little brother Ronny said we'd do the dishes even though Uzi's mum said don't bother. Ronny washed and I dried. I asked him how he's doing 'cause I know he offed not so long ago, and people are usually pretty much in a daze when they get here, at least in the beginning. But Ronny just shrugged and said he thinks OK.

Then he said: 'If it hadn't been for Uzi, I'd have been here a long time ago.'

We did all the dishes and we were putting them away when Ronny started telling me this really weird story about how once, when he was just ten maybe, he took a cab, on his own, to see the two Tel Aviv football teams play each other. He was completely into the yellow team, with the hats and the scarves and everything, and all through the game they were right on top of the other side's goal. Those guys couldn't keep the ball for two passes in a row. But then, eight minutes before the end of the game, the other team scored an offside goal. No two ways about it. It was such an obvious offside – like the replays they show on TV. The yellows tried to argue, but the referee gave the goal and that was that. The other team won, and Ronny went home totally destroyed. Uzi was hung up on fitness in those days. He was going into the army, and he was dead set on trying out for a combat unit. And Ronny, who idolised him, took his skipping rope, tied it to the horizontal bar that Uzi put up in the garden, and made a noose. Then he shouted to Uzi, who was cramming for some final or something, to come right away and told him the whole thing about the game, and about the goal and about how unfair it was and everything, and how he didn't see the point of going on living in a world that's so unfair that the team you love could lose just like that, even when they didn't deserve to. And that he was only telling Uzi because Uzi was probably the cleverest guy Ronny knew, so unless Uzi could give him one good reason to go on living, he was gonna off himself and that was that. The whole time Ronny talked Uzi didn't say a word, and even afterwards, when it was his turn to say something, he just kept quiet, and instead of talking, he took one step forward and slapped Ronny so hard that it sent him flying two yards back, and then he just turned around and went back to his room to do more cramming. Ronny says it took him a while to get over being slapped, but as soon as he got up he untied the rope and put it back and went to have a shower. He never talked to Uzi about the meaning of life again after that.

'I don't know exactly what he was trying to tell me when he slapped me like that,' Ronny said, laughing, and wiped his hands on the dish cloth, 'but whatever it was, it worked fine till the army.'

chapter six

in which Mordy stops barhopping and starts
losing it

I haven't done the bars for almost two weeks. Uzi keeps calling anyway, bugging me about how I'm missing out on the girls and the laughs, and he promises not to bring Kurt along, but so far I'm sitting tight. Once every three days, he even comes to see me at, like, three A.M., helps himself to a beer and tells me some funny story I should've heard at the bar or about some waitress he almost hooked up with. He never leaves anything out, like when some kid misses school and another kid comes over to tell him what they have to do for homework. And then, just before he leaves he tries to talk me into going out for a little espresso before bed. Last night I told him I'd had it with those places, that we never get anywhere with the chicks anyway, and that I just get pissed off.

'As if you're not bummed out anyway,' Uzi goes. 'Look at yourself, vegging in front of the TV every morning like a baboon. Get this, Mordy. The fact that nothing happens is a given. But as long as nothing happens, at least let it be in a place with girls and some music. Right?'

After he left, I tried reading this really depressing book my German roommate lent me – about a guy with TB who went to this place in Italy to spend his dying days. After twenty-three pages I binned it and turned on the TV. They had a game show on, where the contestants meet people who offed on the same date and they all have to say why – but it has to be funny – and what they'd do with the first prize if they won. I figured maybe Uzi was right – just vegging out at home isn't so cool either, and that unless something happened, and soon, I was going to lose it.

chapter seven

in which Mordy accidentally foils a robbery
and almost wins a reward

The day everything began changing
started with me foiling a robbery. I know it sounds
like I'm making it up almost, but it really
happened. I'd just finished buying some stuff at
the supermarket when this fat guy with red hair
and a thick scar on his neck slammed right into
me, and about twenty TV dinners fell out of his
coat. Both of us just froze. I think I was more
shaken up than him.

The cashier next to us yelled: 'Simon! Come
over here, quick. Thief! Thief!'

I wanted to tell the fat guy I was sorry and that
I was happy for him he wasn't really fat. That I
only thought he was on account of the TV dinners
in his coat, and that next time he shoplifts he
should stick to vegetables 'cause meat always
comes out wet and disgusting in the microwave.

But I just shrugged, and the fat guy, who was looking pretty skinny by then, shrugged too, the way only someone with a broken neck can, and then he pegged it. Right after that Simon came running over, waving a stick, and gave this really sad look at the TV dinners that were scattered all over the floor.

'How could he?' he whispered, getting down on his hands and knees, half to me and half to the frozen peas that were rolling all over the place. 'How can anyone do a thing like that? Shoplifting's one thing, but stepping on moussaka?! What good is that?'

Before I could get out of there, the cashier was all over me. 'God, was that lucky! Good thing you were here! Look at him, Simon, this is the guy who caught the thief.'

And Simon's like: 'Terrific,' but he goes on staring at the crushed moussaka. 'Terrific. Superdeal Stores thanks you. If you would be so kind as to step into my office and leave me your name and . . .'

'They'll make it worth your while,' the cashier pitched in. 'There's a reward.'

Simon was busy trying to pick up the TV dinners and work out the damage. I smiled at the cashier and told her thanks a lot, but never mind, and besides I have to be somewhere and I can't wait.

'You sure?' she asked, disappointed. I could tell she was really cut up about it. 'It's a pretty cool reward. A weekend at a hotel.'

When I told Gelfand, he nearly shit a brick.

'A weekend at a hotel?' He peeled himself a banana. 'Couldn't be more obvious than that. The girl's into you.'

'Chill out,' I said. 'It's just store policy.'

'What did she look like?' Gelfand ignored me. 'Was she hot?'

'She was OK, I guess, but . . .'

'No buts,' he insisted. 'Spit it out. How old did she look?'

'Twenty-five,' I gave in.

'Visible scars? Slash marks? Bullet holes, that kinda thing?'

'Not that I could see.'

'A Juliet!' Gelfand whistled in admiration. Juliet's the word they use here for anyone who did it with pills or poison, like me, the ones who get here with no scars. 'Young *and* a Juliet *and* hot too . . .'

'I didn't say she was hot,' I protested.

'C'mon,' Gelfand wouldn't let it go. He put on his disgusting leather piece.

'Where to?' I asked, trying to stall.

'Superdeal,' he announced. 'Let's go and get the reward they owe us.'

'Us?' I asked.

'Just come on and stop chatting,' Gelfand commanded, doing his Mr Big thing. So I shut up and went.

At Superdeal they had a new shift. Simon and the cashier weren't there any more, and the others didn't know what we were talking about. Gelfand tried arguing for a while, but it was becoming a real pain so I went to get us some beers. Next to the carp tank I met Hayim, who was my roomie when I was still alive. I certainly wasn't expecting to see him here. I mean, like, Hayim was just about the sorriest excuse for a human being that I'd ever met, the kind of roommate that could get all pissed off over a couple of hairs in the sink or if you ate some of his cottage cheese. But he was also the last person in the world you'd ever expect to kill himself. I pretended I didn't see him and just kept on going, but he spotted me and shouted, so I had to stop.

'Mordy! I was hoping we'd meet up sooner or later.'

'Hey, man,' I forced a smile. 'Hayim, wassup? What're you doing here?'

'Same as everyone else,' Hayim mumbled. 'Same as everyone else. It's even got something to do with you.'

'What happened?' I asked. 'Did I forget to clean up the kitchen before I offed, or something?'

'You always were a million laughs, Mordy,' Hayim said, and then he went into every detail of how he jumped out the window, straight from our apartment on the fourth floor to the pavement below. And how the whole time he kept hoping it would be over right away, but he fell lopsided – half on a neighbour's car and half on this hedge – and it took, like, hours till it was over. I told him I still didn't get what it had to do with me, and he said it didn't exactly have anything to do with me, but in a way it did.

'Y'know,' he said and arched his back till his head reached the cereal shelf. 'You know how they say suicides always happen in threes. Well, there's something to it. People around you start dying, and you begin to ask yourself what the hell makes you different, and what's keeping you alive, anyway. It hit me like a Scud. I mean I just didn't have the answers. It wasn't you so much, it was more Desiree.'

'Desiree?' I cut in.

'Yeah, Desiree. About a month after you. I was sure you knew.'

Behind the counter, one of the Superdeal workers was whacking this carp on the head with a mallet, and I could feel the tears streaming down my face. I hadn't cried even once since I got here.

'Don't take it so hard,' Hayim said and touched me with his sweaty hand. 'The doctors said she didn't feel a thing. Know what I mean, it was over right away.'

'Who's taking it hard, man?' I kissed him on the forehead. 'She's here, get it? All I gotta do is find her.'

I could see the shift manager in the back, explaining something to Gelfand, who was nodding and looking kind of bored. I guess even he finally figured out we weren't getting any reward.

chapter eight

in which Uzi tries to teach Mordy something
about life and gives up

'You don't have a chance in hell of
finding her,' Gelfand said and helped himself to
a beer. 'I'll bet you anything.'

'A beer,' I smiled and went on packing my
bag.

'A beer,' Gelfand mimicked. 'D'you have any idea
how many bods there are out there, you airhead?
You're clueless. Me and you have been going back
and forth for God knows how long on this two-by-
two piece of shit, and we still don't know half the
people here. So just where are you gonna look for
her? In Kingdom Come? This Genevieve of yours
might be living right next door.'

'Desiree,' I corrected.

'Desiree, Genevieve, Marie-Claire. What's the
difference?' Gelfand opened his beer on a corner
of the table. 'Just another rich chick.'

'Suit yourself,' I answered and went on packing. Last thing I wanted was to pick a fight with him.

'What kind of kinky bourgeois snobs give their daughter a name like that, anyway? Listen, Mordy, if you do find her, you gotta introduce me to her mother.'

'Promise,' I held up my hand. 'Scout's honor.'

'So where are you gonna start looking?' he asked.

I shrugged. 'Desiree always said she hated the city. She wanted to live somewhere more open. With a dog and a garden and everything, you know.'

'That doesn't mean anything,' Gelfand shot back. 'Girls always say that, and then they end up renting a place in a posh part of town with a nerdy roommate. I'm telling you, she could be living right around the corner.'

'I dunno. I've got this really strong hunch that she's not in the city.' I took a quick sip of beer. 'Call it intuition. Worst could happen is we just go for a drive.'

'We?' Gelfand asked, suspicious.

'Figure of speech, that's all,' I reassured him. 'I never thought you'd come with me just to find some rich chick. Besides, I know you've got lots of commitments.'

'Hey, listen,' Gelfand was still at it. 'Don't get smart-assed.'

'I'm not,' I said. 'I just told you. I really wasn't expecting you to come.'

'Gimme, like, one good reason, and I will. It's not like I'm trying to be rude or anything.'

'How about that I love her,' I tried.

'No you don't,' Gelfand shook his head. 'It's just like your stupid suicide. You're all about filling your head with words.'

'No shit. And I guess your suicide was a stroke of genius?'

'I'm not trying to diss you, Mordy. I'm just trying to tell you something. I dunno, like I'm not even sure what it is.' Gelfand sat down beside me. 'Lemme put it this way. Since you got here, how many times d'you get laid?'

'Why?'

'Just because.'

'Actually laid? None, I think.'

'You think?'

'None,' I confessed. 'But what's that got to do with it?'

'Loads. Because you're up to your eyeballs

with sperm, got that? Everything you look at is grey. Your sperm count's so high and your brain's pressing against your skull so hard that you think you're having an out-of-body experience like nobody in the whole damn universe ever had before. Like, you're so strung out it's worth dying for. Leaving everything. Going off to live in the Galilee. Ever live in the Galilee? You know, nothing but goat shit and once-a-day buses.'

'Lay off, Uzi. I really don't need this, you know,' I cut in. 'Just gimme the car, OK? And don't start stressing about the insurance. If I break anything, I'll pay for it.'

'Don't go getting touchy on me all of a sudden,' Gelfand shot back and patted me on the shoulder. 'All I said was that it's not a good enough reason. I didn't say I wouldn't come with you. Maybe you're right. Maybe I'm just bullshitting you. Maybe this Irma really is something special . . .'

'Desiree,' I corrected him again.

'Right,' Gelfand smiled. 'Sorry.'

'Know what? Forget about rich bitches and love and all that shit,' I tried a different tack. 'I've got another reason for you to come.'

'Try me,' Gelfand shot the empty beer bottle in the bin and tried to sound interested.

'You got anything better to do?'

chapter nine

in which the two friends go looking for
Desiree and find Arabs instead

Gelfand promised his parents he'd call
every day, and as soon as we get off he started
looking for a phone.

'Calm down, man,' I told him. 'You've been in
South America, you been in India, you blew your
brains out with a dumdum slug. Stop behaving like
a fucking Boy Scout at summer camp.'

'Get off my case, Mordy. I'm warning you,'
Gelfand snarled and kept driving. 'Just look at
this place. Check out the characters around here.
Tell you the truth, I dunno why I came with
you.'

The people outside looked a lot like the ones in
our neighbourhood – their eyes kinda dim, and
dragging their feet. The only difference was that
Gelfand didn't know them – which was enough to
make him paranoid.

'I'm not being paranoid. Don't you get it? They're all Arabs.'

'So what if they're Arabs?' I asked.

'So what? I dunno. Arabs – suicides – doesn't that psych you out, even a little? What if they figure out we're Israeli?'

'I guess they'll kill us again. Can't you get it into your skull they don't give a flyin' fuck? They're dead. We're dead. *É finita la commedia.*'

'I dunno,' Gelfand muttered. 'I don't like Arabs. It isn't even politics. It's something ethnic.'

'Tell me something, Uzi. Aren't you fucked up enough without being a racist, too?'

'I'm not a racist,' Gelfand squirmed. 'I just . . . know what? Maybe I am a bit racist. But just a bit.'

It was getting dark, and the lights in Gelfand's beat-up old Chevy had been dead for a long time, so we had to stop for the night. He locked the doors from the inside and made us bunk down in the car. We moved the seats back and tried to pretend we were just about to zonk out. Once in a while Uzi even went through the whole toss-and-turn routine. It was really pathetic. After an hour, even he had had enough.

He pulled the seat back up and said: 'C'mon, let's go and find a bar.'

'What about the Arabs?'

'Screw the Arabs,' he said. 'If worst comes to worst, we'll let 'em have it. Like in the army.'

'You were never in the army,' I reminded him. 'You were section eight, which makes sense.'

'Same difference,' Uzi got out of the Chevy and slammed the door. 'I saw how they do it on TV.'

chapter ten

in which Uzi regrets not serving in the army and discovers how hard it is to get dead bods to lose their composure

Turned out Uzi was right. It really was an Arab neighbourhood. But I was right too, because they didn't give a fuck what passports we had before we got here. Their bar was called Djin, which was supposed to be a play on *djinni*, like the one in Aladdin's lamp, and on the stuff that girls and assholes have with tonic when they can't handle scotch. Uzi said it was a lousy pun, but the truth is that after 'Stiff Drinks' anything sounded good. We sat at the bar. The barman looked like he'd offed himself with a vengeance and must have ended up in pieces. Uzi tried English, but the guy picked up on his accent right away and answered in tired Hebrew.

'No bottles, only draught,' he droned. His face was like a puzzle that someone started but gave up in the middle, with part of a moustache to the left of his nose and nothing on the right.

'Give us some draught beer then, bro,' Uzi said and slapped him on the shoulder. 'Let's drink to the good ol' Security Forces, *ya* Muhammed.'

'Nasser,' the barman corrected stiffly and started filling the glasses. 'What's with the Security Forces thing? Were you in the army?' he asked as he poured.

'Sure,' Uzi lied. 'Undercover unit . . . three straight years of battle rations, day in and day out!'

Nasser handed Uzi the beer, and when he brought me mine he whispered: 'He's not all there, your friend, is he?'

'I guess you could say that,' I smiled.

'Never mind,' Nasser reassured me. 'That's why he's so – what's the word? Irresistible.'

'The guy's unreal!' Uzi said and downed half a glass in one go. 'Me – irresistible!'

'He was never really in the army, and it's eating him up,' I explained.

'Yes I was,' Uzi argued. 'I even re-enlisted. The gun –' he said, pointing to the hole in his temple and making like he was shooting a pistol, 'my service weapon. So, Nasser, how'd you close up shop?' Uzi was obviously trying to pick a fight, 'cause if there's one thing you're never supposed to ask around here it's how they offed. But this Nasser guy looked so wasted that even Uzi couldn't rattle him.

'Kaboom!' he smiled faintly and wiggled his mangled body a little. 'Can't you tell?'

'No shit,' Uzi said. 'Kaboom! How many'd you take with you?' Nasser shook his head and poured himself a vodka.

'How should I know?'

'You're pulling my leg,' Uzi was a bit freaked out. 'You never even asked? Somebody must have got after you.'

'It's not the kind of thing you ask,' Nasser said and downed the shot of vodka.

'Tell me where and when it was,' Uzi nagged. 'If I was after you, maybe I could tell you how many . . .'

'Drop it,' Nasser stiffened for a moment.

'What for?'

'Hey,' I made a move to change the subject, 'it's packed here tonight.'

'Yeah, dynamite,' Nasser smiled. 'It's like this every night. Trouble is it's almost all guys. Every once in a while you get a couple of girls. A tourist maybe. But hardly any.'

'Hey,' Uzi pressed on, 'is it true that when you people go out on a job they promise you seventy nymphomaniac virgins in Kingdom Come? All for you, *solico*?'

'Sure, they promise,' Nasser said, 'and look what it got me. Lukewarm vodka.'

'So you're just a sucker in the end, eh, *ya* Nasser,' Uzi gloated.

'Sure thing,' Nasser nodded. 'And you, what did they promise you?'

chapter eleven

in which Mordy dreams about him and
Desiree buying a sofa, and has a rude
awakening

That night, in the car, I dreamed that
Desiree and me are buying a sofa, and the salesman
is the Arab from the bar, the one Uzi kept hassling.
He shows us all kinds of sofas, and we can't decide
on one we both like. The one Desiree wants is
really gross, with red upholstery and everything,
and I want something else – I can't remember
what, exactly. And we get into an argument right
there in the shop. We're not just discussing it.
We're yelling. And it gets uglier and uglier, and
we start saying things that really hurt, and then,
in the dream, suddenly I get hold of myself and
I stop short.

'Let's not fight,' I say. 'It doesn't matter. Just a
stupid sofa, that's all. The only thing that matters
is that we're together.' And when I say it, she smiles,

and then, instead of smiling back, I wake up in the car. Uzi's on the seat next to me, and he's tossing and turning in his sleep, cursing all sorts of people who were bugging him in his dream.

'Shut it,' he was telling someone who must have really gone too far. 'One more word and you'll have a mud pie on your head.' I guess the guy just kept going, 'cause Uzi tried to get up and caught the steering wheel in the ribs. With him awake too, we opened the windows and had a smoke.

'Tomorrow we're getting a wigwam or an igloo, or whatever you call that piece of plastic shit they sell at camping supplies shops,' Uzi announced.

'A tent,' I said.

'Yeah, a tent. That's the last time we sleep in the car.' Uzi took one more puff and threw the butt out the window. 'He was an OK guy, actually, that Arab in the bar. The beer was shit but that Nasser was pretty sharp. You know what I was dreaming about?'

'Yeah,' I said and took a drag of what was left of my cigarette, 'that you're crapping on his head.'

chapter twelve

in which the guys give a girl a ride and try to
make conversation

The next morning me and Uzi picked
up this hitchhiker, which was kind of weird if you
stop and think about it, because nobody hitches
rides around here. Uzi spotted her from a distance.

'Holy shit! What a piece of ass,' he muttered
under his breath.

'A Juliet?' I asked with my eyes half shut.

'A jewel of a Juliet!' he said, all hyped up. 'I
swear to you, Mordy, a girl like that, if we weren't
seeing her here, I'd never guess she offed herself.'

Uzi always gets spazzed out when he's horny,
but this time he was really on the money. There
was something full of life in her eyes that you
don't see much around here. After we passed her,
I went on looking in the wing mirror – long black
hair and a backpack like hikers use – and suddenly
I saw her stick out her thumb. Uzi saw it too and

hit the brakes. The car behind us almost bashed our brains in but managed to swerve past us at the last second. Uzi backed up, till we were right next to her.

'Hop on in, sis,' he said, trying to sound totally cool, but it didn't really work.

'Where you heading?' she asked suspiciously.

'East,' I said.

'East where?' she asked again, tossing her backpack on the back seat and climbing in.

I shrugged.

'You got a clue where you're going?'

'You haven't been here long, I guess,' Uzi laughed.

'Why's that?' she asked, kinda pissed off.

''Cause otherwise you'd've figured out by now that nobody here has a clue. Maybe if we did, we wouldn't be here in the first place.'

Her name was Leehee, and she told us that she really did just get here and that she's been hitching the whole time, because she's gotta find the people in charge.

'The people in charge?!' Uzi laughed. 'What do you think this is, a sodding country club, where you go to the main office? This place is just like before you offed, only a little bit worse. By the way, when you were still alive, d'you ever go looking for God?'

'No,' Leehee said and offered me some chewing gum. 'But I didn't really have any reason to.'

'And what reason do you have now?' Uzi laughed and took some gum too. 'You're sorry you did it? 'Cause you know, if that's it, and you're all ready with your backpack and everything and you're just waiting for someone to hand you the visa back home . . .'

'Tell me,' I butted in before he started getting really mean. 'Why'd you wait till we passed you before you stuck out your thumb?'

'I don't know,' Leehee shrugged. 'I guess I wasn't sure I wanted to hitch a ride with you. When I saw you from far away I thought you looked a little . . .'

'Mean?' Uzi suggested.

'No,' Leehee smiled awkwardly. 'Obnoxious.'

chapter thirteen

in which Mordy continues to not lose hope,
Uzi to complain, and Leehee to keep her
sleeves down

It's been five days since we picked up
Leehee. Uzi still keeps stashing small change and
looking for phone booths all day long. Not a fucking
day goes by when he doesn't talk to his parents
for at least an hour, and when me or Leehee tease
him about it, he gets all uptight. At least he's
stopped bugging us about the insurance, so now
the three of us can take turns driving. We make
pretty good time even though we can't drive at
night 'cause the headlights don't work. Around us
there's less and less city, fewer people and more
sky, more little houses with gardens, though
somehow everything's always wilted. The tent was
a pretty good deal and we're getting kinda used
to it. Every night I have that stupid dream about
the fight with Desiree, and every night we make

up, and suddenly I'm awake and Uzi's telling me there's no way we're ever gonna find her, but that he doesn't mind going on until I give up. He always goes out of his way to talk about Desiree when Leehee's around. Leehee thinks I do have a chance, but Uzi doesn't think much of her anyway. Yesterday when we stopped to have a piss, he started bitching that ever since she joined us everything had been getting a bit serious.

'Neither one of us is gonna score with her anyway, y'know,' he said and wrung it out. 'But at least when we were on our own we could play around.'

'Play around all you want,' I said. 'Who's stopping you?'

'Basically you're right,' Uzi admitted, 'but deep down we both know that chatting up chicks just isn't the same when there's a girl around. Somehow it always sounds less like you mean it and more like you're all talk.'

When we got back to the car, I took over the wheel. All this time, Leehee was asleep in her hoodie in the back seat. From the time we picked her up, I'd never seen her wearing anything with short sleeves. Uzi said he'd bet the Chevy she slashed her wrists, but neither of us had the guts to ask her how she offed and everything, and why. Not that it matters much. She's cute when she's sleeping, kind of peaceful, and except for the bit about finding the people in charge, which is a bit nuts if you ask me, she's cool. Uzi can go on bitching all he wants, but personally I think he's got a thing for her. Maybe that's really why he doesn't let it go, so I don't catch on. Truth is, sometimes I think about it myself, that maybe I won't ever find Desiree, and that maybe Leehee will fall in love with me a little too, but I snap out of it right away. Anyway, I have this hunch that Desiree's really close. Uzi says that's a load of crap, that she's probably way on the other side, and that wherever she is, she's bound to have someone by now, probably some black guy who hanged himself by his dick. But I can practically smell how close she is, and how I'm gonna find her, and just because the best friend I've got here is totally losing it, that doesn't mean I have to lose it too.

chapter fourteen

which begins with a miracle and ends with a close call

That evening, just when we were starting to look for a place to stop, the weirdest thing happened. Leehee was at the wheel when suddenly this truck tried to overtake us. The guy leaned on the horn and scared the shit out of us. Leehee skidded off the road to let the truck pass, but then, just when she signalled to get back on the road, the headlights went on all of a sudden. Uzi, who was sitting in the back, was, like, totally psyched.

'You're in-fuckin-credible! You're a genius!' he said and he kissed her so hard she almost lost her grip on the wheel. 'You're the Florence Nightingale of vehicles. Forget Nightingale. You're Marie Curie. You're Golda Meir.'

'Chill out, will you,' she laughed. 'It's only the headlights.'

43

'Only the headlights?!' Uzi looked at Leehee like he was feeling sorry for her. 'God, you're so naive. I don't know what you're more of – naive or brilliant. D'you have any idea how many mechanics got under the hood of this old banger? Forget mechanics. Nuclear engineers, holistic healers of heavy machinery, people who can take apart a Mack diesel engine and put it back together again in twenty seconds blindfolded couldn't fix it, till you got here.' He was massaging her neck. 'My angel genius.' From where I sat it looked like Uzi'd chilled a little by then and he was just using the chance to go on pawing her.

'You know what this means?' I said. 'It means we can keep on driving at night now, too.'

'No shit!' Uzi said. 'And the first place we go tonight with these painfully beautiful headlights is to get wasted.'

We kept on going, looking for a bar. Once you got out of town, things were a bit dead. Every half hour or so we'd pass a sign for some burger bar or pizza place.

After four hours Uzi'd had it, and we stopped to celebrate at this place that sold ice cream and frozen yogurt. Uzi asked what they had that was the closest to alcohol, and the salesgirl said it was cherry liqueur ice cream.

'Hey, Sandra,' Uzi said after he took a peek at her name badge, 'how many cones d'you think we'd have to have to really get wasted?'

Under her name on the badge was their logo – a seal in a clown's hat riding a unicycle, and under that was the motto: 'Low in price, high in flavour.'

'I dunno,' Sandra shrugged.

'Then give us ten pints,' Uzi said. 'Just to be sure.'

Sandra was really good at filling the containers. She looked kind of worn out, but her eyes were wide open the whole time, almost like she was constantly surprised. Whatever she did to off herself, it must have been sudden. On our way to the car, Leehee stopped next to this poster listing all the things the workers were supposed to remember: Be polite to customers. Wash your hands after using the bathroom. That kind of thing. We had one like that at the Kamikaze, right next to the loo, and I never washed my hands when I had a shit. No reason – just to feel like I was doing my own thing.

'Places like that really get me down,' Leehee

said back in the car, after we'd had some of the ice cream. 'I go in hoping something unexpected will happen. Something small even. Like a salesperson wearing a name tag upside down or forgetting to put on a hat, or just going, "Give yourself a break – the food here really sucks." But it never actually happens. Know what I mean?'

'Frankly,' Uzi grabbed the ice cream away from her, 'not really. Want me to drive?' You could tell he was dying to take the wheel, with the new lights and everything. Less than a mile after he took over, there was a sharp turn to the right and just beyond it was this tall, thin guy with glasses sprawled right in the middle of the road, fast asleep. He went right on snoring – even after Uzi swerved off the road and wrapped the car around a tree. We got out. Nobody was hurt, but the Chevy was a total wreck.

'Hey, you,' Uzi screamed, running toward the guy and shaking him. 'You crazy or something?'

'Vice versa,' he said. In, like, a second, the guy was wide awake and up on his feet. He held out his hand to Uzi. 'I'm Raphael. Raphael Kneller. But you guys can call me Rafi.' When he saw that Uzi wasn't taking his hand, he squinted and asked: 'What's that smell? Like ice cream.' And right after that, without waiting for an answer: 'You haven't seen a dog around here by any chance, have you?'

chapter fifteen

in which Kneller extends lots of hospitality and
a little paranoia, and explains why his house
isn't really a camp

After Uzi'd calmed down a little, we
checked out the car and saw it was totalled. Kneller
was shaken up 'cause of what happened and 'cause
it was all his fault. He said he wanted us to come
and crash at his place anyway. He didn't stop blab-
bing the whole way, and every step he took, his body
went all over the place like he was trying to go in
several directions at the same time and couldn't
make up his mind. One thing's for sure, he looked
completely crazy, this Kneller, but harmless. He even
smelled kinda fresh and innocent, like a baby's
bottom. I couldn't picture a guy like that offing
himself.

'I'm not usually out at this hour, but I was looking
for my dog, Freddie. He's lost. D'you see him by
any chance? It's just that suddenly all the peace and

quiet around here started really getting to me. Well, what d'you expect? Everyone likes to veg out in the woods, know what I mean, in the great outdoors and everything.' Kneller tried to explain, waving his arms around a lot.

'But why that way? Why in the middle of the fucking road, dammit? I mean it's fucking irresponsible, if you ask me.'

'Too many recreational drugs, I guess,' he winked at us, and when he saw that Uzi was still really pissed off and looking pretty peeved, he added quickly: 'Metaphorically, I mean. Nobody really does drugs around here.'

Kneller's house looked just like those stupid little houses we used to draw in kindergarten, with a red roof and a chimney, a green tree in the garden and a yellowish light in the windows. There was an enormous sign over the doorway, with FOR RENT on it in big bold letters, and KNELLER'S HAPPY CAMPERS scribbled in blue paint right over that. Kneller told us that the house wasn't really for rent, or actually, that it used to be for rent once but that then Kneller came along and rented it, and it isn't like he even runs a camp. It's just a joke, not a very funny one, that a friend of his made up. This friend used to live with him for a

49

Etgar Keret

long time, and he thought because of all the company that kept coming and all the fun stuff that Kneller used to set up for them, that this place was kind of like a camp.

'Wait till they see the ice cream,' he smiled, and he pointed to the container that Leehee was holding. 'They'll freak out.'

chapter sixteen

in which Leehee performs a small miracle and Uzi falls in love with an Eskimo

It's been almost a month since we got here. Kneller's starting to get used to the idea that his dog Freddie isn't planning to come back, and it doesn't look like the tow truck that Gelfand ordered is ever going to show up either. During the first week, Uzi was still driving everybody crazy and dialing all sorts of numbers to figure out a way of getting back home, but then he met this Eskimo. She was seriously cute and was from too far away to pick up on his character. Ever since they've been an item he's less hung up on getting out of here, and even though he still calls his mum and dad every day, now mostly he talks about her. At first this place really got to me, too, with its cheerleader types from all over, who only after they offed discovered that this place was actually the flip side of fun. Kind of like a cross between

United Colors of Benetton and Swiss Family Robinson. Except that the people here are really nice. Kind of dazed but doing their best to get the most out of the little spark they have, even if it's not much. Then there's Kneller, who's all over the place, waving his arms like he's conducting an orchestra. I told Leehee that when I was in high school we had a question in our physics book about this guy, Mr Magic they called him, who falls off the roof of a building and uses a stopwatch to see how long it takes. It didn't say there what he looked like, but somehow I'd pictured him like Kneller. Really into it, but way out. Leehee asked me how the physics question ended, and I told her I couldn't remember, but I bet Mr Magic was saved in the end, because it's a physics book for kids and everything. And Leehee told me if that's true, then it had to be Kneller, because she could easily picture him walking off the roof of a building, but there was no way she could see him actually hitting the ground.

The next morning we went along to help him out in the garden. So far he hasn't managed to grow anything there except weed. After we'd worked for a while, Leehee turned on the tap to get a drink, and instead of water she got soda.

Leehee and me got pretty worked up about that, but Kneller wasn't impressed.

'Don't pay any attention,' he said indifferently. 'Happens all the time around here.'

'What does?' I asked.

'Things like that,' Kneller went on hoeing the flowerbeds.

'Miracles?' I asked. 'Because you know, Rafi, it isn't like Leehee turned water into wine, but it comes pretty close.'

'Not close enough,' Kneller said. 'You wanna give it a name? Call it a miracle, but it's not a significant one. Miracles like that are no biggie around here. Strange you even noticed. Most people don't.'

Leehee and I didn't really get it. But Kneller explained that one of the things about this place was that people can do pretty amazing stuff like turning stones into plants, or changing animals' colours, or even floating in the air a bit. But only so long as it's not significant and it doesn't count for anything. I told him that was pretty amazing and that if it was really happening so much around here, then we could try putting together some kind of a show, like a magic act or something, maybe even getting it on television.

'But that's what I'm trying to tell you,' Kneller said and kept scuffing the ground. 'You can't do that, 'cause as soon as people come specially to see it, it won't work. These things only work if they don't really matter. It's like, say, you find yourself suddenly walking on water, which is something that happens here every now and then, but only if there's nothing waiting for you on the other side, or if there's no one around who's gonna get all worked up about it.'

Leehee told him about what happened to the headlights the night we met, and Kneller said it was a perfect example.

'Fixing the headlights of a car sounds pretty significant to me,' I objected.

'Depends where you're going,' Kneller smiled. 'If you end up wrapping it around a tree five minutes later, then not really.'

chapter seventeen

in which Leehee tells Mordy something
intimate and Uzi insists it's just a load of shit

Ever since Kneller and me had that talk,
I began paying more attention to miracles.
Yesterday I was on a walk with Leehee, and she
stopped for a second to tie her laces. Suddenly,
just like that, the rock that she put her foot on
started falling upside down toward the sky and
disappeared out of sight, for no reason. And the
day before that, when Uzi was about to rack up
the pool balls, one of them suddenly turned into
an egg. Truth is, I'm dying to perform my first
miracle too, any kind of miracle, even if it's a
really dumb one. Kneller says that so long as I
want it really badly it's like something important,
and that's why I'll never get it to work. Maybe
he's right, but there's something really mixed up
and spacey about his whole explanation.

Kneller says it's not his explanation. It's 'cause

55

this whole place doesn't really make sense. One minute you're offing yourself, and the next thing you know – wham! – there you are with scars and a mortgage. And why only suicides, anyway? Why not normal dead people too? Like, somehow the whole thing doesn't make any sense. Take it or shove it, know what I mean? And even if it's not that groovy, things could've been a lot worse. Uzi's spending all his time with his new girlfriend. There's this river not far from here, and she's teaching him how to kayak and fish, which is pretty weird, 'cause I for one never heard or saw any animals around here practically, except for Kneller's dog maybe. And for all I know that dog may not even exist, either. Uzi doesn't have much to offer her in return, but just so he doesn't feel like a schmuck he's teaching her the names of all the late greats of football, and how to swear in Arabic. And me – most of the time I'm with Leehee. Kneller's got these bikes in his storeroom, and we go cycling a lot. She told me about how she offed. Turns out she didn't kill herself at all. She just ODed. Somebody talked her into shooting up. It was the first time for both of them, and they probably botched it. That's why she's convinced it's all a mistake and that if she could just find one of the people in charge and explain, they'd transfer her out of here right away. Truth is, I don't think she has a chance of finding anyone like that, but I think I'd better not tell her. Leehee asked me not to talk about it to anyone but I told Uzi, and Uzi said it was a load of shit and that nobody gets here by mistake. I told him what Kneller says about how this whole place is one big mistake and that if the place is so flaky that a pool ball can turn into an egg, then why couldn't it also be true that Leehee got here by mistake.

'Y'know what this reminds me of?' Uzi mumbled, stuffing his face with a toasted-cheese sandwich. 'It reminds me of those movies where they throw the good guy in the slammer and all those other people keep telling him how they're there by mistake and that they're really innocent but you take one look at them and you can see they're guilty as hell. You know I really like Leehee but what's all this crap about OD'ing? D'you ever see anyone in Tel Aviv shoot up? They piss themselves about a tetanus shot. They see a needle and pass out.'

'It's not like she's a druggie or anything,' I said. 'It was her first time.'

57

Etgar Keret

'Her first time?' Uzi took a sip of his coffee. 'Believe me, Mordy, nobody dies from a first time, no matter of what, unless they seriously want to.'

chapter eighteen

in which Mordy dreams he's in a prison film
with a bad ending, all because he doesn't
have character

That night I dreamed that Uzi and
Leehee and me were breaking out of prison.
Getting out of the cell was pretty easy, but once
we got to the yard, there were all these sirens and
floodlights and stuff. The van was waiting for us
on the other side, and I helped lift Uzi and Leehee
to climb over. But when I wanted to climb over
myself, there was nobody left to help me, and then
suddenly I see Kneller, and before I can even ask
him, he just floats up in the air and over to the
other side. Everybody's out by then, including
Desiree, who's driving the van, and they're all just
waiting for me. I can hear the sirens and the dogs
behind me, and all the other stuff you always hear
in prison films, and they're closing in on me. And
Uzi keeps screaming at me from the other side:

'Shit, Mordy, what is it with you? Just float a bit.' And just to piss me off, Kneller keeps floating back and forth over the van, doing all kinds of loops and back-flips and stuff, and I try too but I just can't cut it. Then they all drive off, or else Uzi's family shows up. Truth is, I don't really remember what happens after that.

'You know what that dream's trying to tell you?' Uzi says. 'That you're screwed up. A pushover, and screwed up too. A pushover, because all I have to do is say the word 'slammer' once, and you go and have a dream about it. And screwed up, 'cause that's what the dream itself says.'

Uzi and me are sitting by the river holding a clothesline and trying to fish with some trick his girlfriend taught him. We've been sitting there for, like, two hours, and nothing. Not even a fucking shoe, which is what's really pissing him off.

'Just think about it. In your dream, everyone gets out 'cause they don't take their existence seriously. But you, you're so busy obsessing that you're just stuck. That dream's open and shut. Almost educational, if you ask me.'

It's getting cold, and I'm beginning to wonder when Uzi will ever get tired of this fishing shit, 'cause to tell the truth, I got fed up a long time ago, and it's pretty obvious there are no fish here.

'Let me tell you something else,' Uzi went on. 'It's not just your dream. It's that you remember it and go on about it. There's lots of people with dreams but they don't get all stressed out. I have dreams too, y'know, but I don't go making you listen to them, and that's why I'm a happier person.' And then, like he has to prove his point, he gives his line a pull, and there's this fish at the end of it. Small and ugly but big enough to inflate Uzi's overinflated ego even more. 'Listen to a friend for a change. Forget your dumb dreams and those stupid miracles. Now's the knowing. Go for Leehee. Why not? She looks good. A bit spacey maybe but nice, and she likes you, that's obvious. Take it from me, she's never going to find God and file her complaint, and you're never going to find your rich chick. You're both stuck here on your own, so you might as well make the most of it.'

The ugly fish was squirming on Uzi's line. Suddenly it changed into something else, red and a little bigger but just as ugly. Uzi held it down and bashed its head with a stone to make it stop flopping, which is another Eskimo trick. He didn't even notice how it changed. To tell the truth, maybe he's right. Maybe it really doesn't fucking matter. But when it comes to Desiree, I just know she's here. It's like all I have to do is turn around and she'll be there behind me. And I don't give a shit how much Uzi teases me, 'cause I just know I'm going to find her.

'Tell me one thing,' Uzi says on our way home. 'This Kneller, what is going on with him? Why is he always so fucking happy, and hugging people and stuff? Is he gay or what?'

chapter nineteen

in which Kneller has a birthday party and
Mordy and Leehee decide to move on

More and more people keep arriving,
'cause Kneller's supposed to be having this
birthday blast and everyone's all psyched up –
baking cakes or dreaming up far-out things to give
him. Most of them are so uncoordinated you
wonder how they even breathe, and Leehee says
we'll be damn lucky if all this creative hullabaloo
doesn't get anyone hurt. So far, two of them cut
themselves and another guy is bleeding from every
finger 'cause he was trying to sew Kneller a bag.
And then there's this Dutch space cadet, Jan.
Yesterday he grabbed a butterfly net and said he
was going to catch Kneller a new dog in the woods.
Hasn't been heard from since. Kneller's happy as
a pig in shit. In the evening, we were setting the
table for this blowout meal, and I asked him how
old he was, and he started to kind of stutter, 'cause

suddenly he discovered he couldn't remember. After all the food and the presents, they played some CDs and people actually danced, like it was a fucking disco or something. I even slow-danced with Leehee. At about four in the morning, someone remembered that Kneller used to play the fiddle and that his old violin was just lying there in the storeroom. At first he wouldn't play, but pretty soon he gave in and played 'Knockin' on Heaven's Door'. Truth is, I don't know shit about music, but I never in my life heard anyone play like that. It's not that he didn't miss a couple of notes. He did. But you could tell by the sound that he was really sincere about what he was playing. It wasn't only me. Everyone just stood there and listened and didn't say a word, like when there's a moment of silence for someone that died. Even Uzi, the original killjoy, kept quiet, and his eyes were watery. He told me later it was his allergies, but you could see he was just saying that. After Kneller finished playing, nobody wanted to do much any more. Mostly they just hit the sack, and Leehee and me helped clean up a bit. In the kitchen she asked me if I still miss all the things from before I offed. I told her the truth, that it isn't like I'm not dying to go back, but I don't remember much of anything except Desiree, and now that she's here too, there's nothing I miss.

'Maybe I miss myself a little,' I said. 'The way I used to be before I offed. I'm probably just making this up, but I remember myself more like . . . I don't know. I can't even remember that any more.'

Leehee said she missed everything, even the things she hated, and that she had to work out how to take off by the following day, because the only way she was ever going to find someone who could help her was to keep looking. I told her she was right and that I should pack up, too, if I really wanted to find Desiree. We finished stacking the dishes in the sink, but neither of us really wanted to call it a night yet. Kneller was sitting on the living-room floor, playing with his presents like some kid. Suddenly Jan came in, all worked up, holding his ridiculous butterfly net, and said that the Messiah King was living on the other side of the forest and that he was holding Kneller's dog hostage.

chapter twenty

in which Freddie packs away some kebabs
and uses an alias

Jan stared at us, out of breath and red
and everything. We sat him down in the living room
and brought him a glass of water and he told us
how he got lost in the forest looking for a new dog
for Kneller, and how in the end, when he came out
on the other side, he saw this mansion with a swimming pool and he wanted to ask the people there
to let him use the phone to call Kneller's place so
that he could ask us to send someone to pick him
up, but there was no phone in the mansion, just
lots of music and noise, and everyone there had a
ponytail and a suntan and they all looked Australian
except the girls in thongs. They were really nice
and gave Jan loads of food to eat and told him that
the mansion belonged to the Messiah King and
that all of them were in his crowd and that the
Messiah King only liked techno, which was why

that was the only thing they kept playing, and full blast. They said the Messiah King was also called Joshua, but everyone there called him J, 'cause one of the girls called him that once and it stuck, and that J was originally from some back-of-beyond little place in the Galilee, but that he's been here for ever, and there was going to be a significant miracle in a week. A planned miracle. Not something that just happened by chance. And that they couldn't say what it was but that it would be something majorly big and that Jan could stay and watch. Jan was kinda getting used to the music and was sort of into it by then, partly because of the miracle, but mainly because of all the naked girls. They got him a room in the mansion with this really nice surfer who, before he offed himself, was manager of the Hard Rock Café in Wellington, New Zealand. That evening they all went skinny-dipping and Jan was kinda shy so he just stood next to the pool, but suddenly he spotted Kneller's dog, Freddie, eating kebabs from a plastic dish. Jan explained that Freddie belonged to a good friend of his and that he'd been lost for a few weeks, and everyone seemed pretty confused because the Messiah King had adopted the dog and said that it was really brainy and that he even taught it to talk. Jan knew the dog could say a few words even though it didn't really understand them, anyway. But he also knew that apart from that the dog was really dim, but he didn't want to say so because he didn't want to make the Messiah King look bad.

This Messiah King, J, was a tall, blue-eyed blond guy with long hair, and he had this girlfriend who was a little lopsided but pretty anyway, and they both listened patiently to Jan's story. Then finally J said that if the dog was lost, he'd give it back for sure, and that there was a really simple way of finding out. He asked Jan for the dog's name, and Jan said Freddie, and then J called Freddie, who'd just finished eating, and asked him what his name was, and the dumb dog wagged its tail and said: 'Saddam,' which was a really lame joke that Freddie learned when he was just a puppy from this marine who offed himself in the middle of an officer training course and spent some time at Kneller's. Jan tried to explain, but J was already positive it wasn't the same dog, and Freddie was making all kinds of signs like he didn't want to go off with Jan because Kneller would never in his life give him kebabs. So Jan thought the best thing would be to get back here and tell us everything.

'Messiah King – significant miracles – trance!'

Kneller was totally pissed off. 'The whole thing sounds like a load of crap to me. The only thing that doesn't surprise me at all is that Freddie didn't want to come back. I always said he was an ingrate.'

chapter twenty-one

in which Mordy and Leehee set out in search
of the Messiah King and find the sea by
mistake

At seven the next morning, when most of
the guests were still passed out on the carpet,
Kneller picked up his backpack and stood there
in the middle of the living room and said he
couldn't wait any more. He wanted to see Freddie
right away. Leehee and me offered to tag along.
Leehee didn't exactly buy into the whole Messiah
King thing, but she thought she had nothing to
lose by asking him about the people in charge and
how she could find them. And I thought if there
really were as many people there as Jan said, then
maybe it could be a good place to look for Desiree.
Besides, Kneller and Jan were both so fucking
uncoordinated that it wouldn't be a bad idea to
have someone keep an eye on them. Kneller
wanted us to use a bus that belonged to one of

his friends, but Jan said he only knew how to get to this place on foot. Which is why we had to string along behind him through the forest for more than ten hours, till it started turning dark. That's when he had to admit he was lost. Kneller said it was a good sign, because Jan got lost last time too, and to celebrate he took out this bong, and him and Jan each took four hits, till they were totally wasted. Leehee and me decided to get some twigs to light a fire. All we had was the lighter we took from Kneller, who was sleeping like a baby. As soon as we moved away from him and Jan, who was snoring next to him, we started hearing a different sound, in the distance, like something that was breaking but was soothing too, and Leehee said it sounded to her like the sea. We headed toward it, and sure enough – a few hundred yards later we reached the beach. It was really bizarre that nobody at the camp, not even Kneller himself, ever mentioned we were near the beach. Could be they didn't know it themselves. Could be we were the only ones who knew. We took our shoes off and walked a while along the beach. Before I offed, I used to go to the beach a lot, almost every day. And when I thought about it, I got a better idea about what Leehee was saying last night –

about missing things and having to go back. I told Leehee about Uzi's dad, who calls this place Deadsville, and about how the people here all seem like they don't want anything, and that most of the time when you're next to them it feels like everything is OK, when actually you're half dead already. And Leehee laughed and said that most of the people she knew, even before she offed, were either half dead or completely dead, so I was in pretty good shape. And when she said it she touched me, like it was just by accident, but it wasn't really.

I'd always hoped that if I ever cheated on Desiree, it would be with someone really pretty, so that later, when I regretted it, I could tell myself she was so beautiful that nobody would've been able to resist her. Truth is that's just how Leehee was. And that night, when she touched me, I knew she was right and that I was in pretty good shape actually.

chapter twenty-two

in which Kneller tells Freddie the whole truth
to his face

Leehee and me woke up at sunrise.
Actually, we woke up 'cause Kneller was screaming.
As soon as we opened our eyes, we saw the beach
around us wasn't private any more. Not that there
were any people around, but now, in daylight, we
discovered the whole place was covered with used
condoms. Floating in the shallow water like jelly-
fish or stuck in the sand like oysters. And suddenly
everything began to smell of used rubber.
Somehow it all got swallowed up by the smell of
the sea the night before. I had to stop myself from
puking, because of Leehee. I held her very close
to me, and we just lay there like that, without
moving, for I don't know how long, like a couple
of tourists stranded in a minefield, waiting to be
rescued.

'There you are,' suddenly Kneller just popped

out from between the trees. 'I was getting really worried. Why don't you answer when people call you?'

He led us back to where he and Jan spent the night, and he explained on the way that this beach used to be a hangout for hookers and druggies, except it became so grim that even hookers and druggies couldn't take it.

'Don't tell me you actually spent the night here,' he said and made a face like he couldn't believe it. Meanwhile Leehee and me wiped off the sand and everything that was sticking to our clothes. 'What the hell for?'

'That's how it is when you love the beach,' Leehee said, giving him her half-smile.

'That's how it is when you love diseases,' Kneller corrected her without skipping a beat. 'Just let's hope Jan doesn't get lost on us now.'

Sure enough, Jan was gone, but before we could start worrying about him, he came running toward us, looking totally ecstatic, and said he'd finally found the Messiah King's house and that it was really close.

The Messiah King's place was humongous, like all those cool houses that Desiree used to show me when we visited her rich relatives in Caesarea.

The kind of place where besides the swimming pool they have a squash court and a Jacuzzi, and a fallout shelter in the basement, just in case. There were more than a hundred people standing around when we got there, in a kind of a half-cocktail, half-buffet thing that must've been going on since the day before, with a lot of New Agey types, plenty of surfers, and all kinds of other characters, and everybody seemed really wired. Freddie kept making the rounds, pulling pitiful faces, forcing everyone to feed him, and as soon as Kneller saw him he just freaked out. He stood there facing Freddie and started yelling about how could he treat him that way, and on his birthday no less, and that he was an ingrate. He started bringing up all sorts of embarrassing things that had happened when Freddie was still a pup. And all that time Freddie just looked at him calmly and went on stuffing his face on this piece of sushi like some old geezer with chewing tobacco. Everyone tried to get Kneller to cool it and to tell him that J would arrive in a minute and fix everything. And when they saw it wasn't doing any good, they tried to get him interested in the miracle that J was about to perform, which only got him more hysterical. Meanwhile Leehee and me were helping ourselves to the finger food, 'cause we hadn't eaten all morning. There was a lot we wanted to say and we pretended we weren't saying it because of the racket but we knew that wasn't the real reason. Then Jan arrived and said that J and his girlfriend wanted Kneller and Freddie to come to see them in the living room to find out what this was all about, and that we'd better come too because Kneller swore he was going to raise hell. Even before we got there we could hear Kneller screaming, and there was this low doggish voice mumbling every now and then: 'Cool it, man, cool it.' I could pick out Desiree's voice too.

I don't know how many times I'd pictured that moment. A million at least. The ending was always cool. Not that I didn't imagine any complications. I'd thought of all of them so that no matter what happened, no matter what she said, I'd be ready. Desiree recognised me right away. She ran up and hugged me and started crying. Then she introduced me to J, who shook my hand and said he'd heard a lot about me, and seemed like an OK guy. And I introduced her to Leehee, which was kind of embarrassing. Leehee didn't say anything but I could tell that even though it was sort of complicated she was happy for me. We left everyone behind and went out on the balcony. Through the door we could hear Kneller ranting, and J, who must have given up on Freddie long ago, mumbling something like he agreed. Desiree told me about what happened after I offed, about

77

how she didn't know what to do with herself, about how she felt so guilty she wanted to die. And the whole time she talked I just looked at her, at how she looked just the way I remembered her – same haircut even – except her posture, which was kind of bizarre, because she offed by jumping from the roof of the Tiberias Hospital. Desiree told me how after my funeral she went up to the Galilee and the whole way she just cried and cried. Then, when she got to the final stop, the first thing she saw was Joshua, and as soon as she saw him something inside her became calmer, and she just stopped crying. It's not that she stopped being sad, but it wasn't hysterical any more. It was just as deep, but something she could deal with. Joshua believed that we were all trapped in the world of the living and that there was a better world that he could get to and there were a few others who believed in his powers. Two weeks after she and Joshua met, he was supposed to separate his body from his soul, to discover the other world and to return and show everyone the way. Except that something got screwed up and his soul never made it back. At the hospital, after they'd confirmed his death, she could feel him calling her from wherever he was, which is when she took the lift up to the roof and jumped, so that they could be together. And now they were, and Joshua was going to do it again – what he'd tried to do in the Galilee – except that this time she was sure he'd make it and that he'd find the way and he'd come back and show everyone. Then she told me again how much I meant to her, and that she knew she hurt me. She didn't know how much until after I offed, and she's glad she got to see me again so that she could ask me to forgive her. And all that time I just smiled and nodded. Whenever I'd picture us talking about it, there were plenty of times when I saw her with someone else, but I always used to fight. I'd tell her how much I love her, that nobody could love her that way, and I'd hug her and touch her till she gave in. But now that it was really happening, out here on the terrace, all I wanted was to get to the part where she gave me the friendly kiss on the cheek and it would be over. And then, as if to save me, there was a gong, and Desiree explained that it was time to go back, because it meant that Joshua was about to begin, and she just hugged me instead.

chapter twenty-four

in which J promises to perform a significant miracle

When we got back inside, Leehee and Kneller were gone. J, who was wearing this fancy gown with lots of embroidery, said they were downstairs already, and when I went looking for them by the pool I saw that the crowd had split, the guys on one side and the girls on the other. I found Kneller right away, and I could see Leehee in the distance, too. She was making signs like to ask me how it went. I couldn't think of any way to signal what had happened with Desiree. I wanted to tell her from a distance that I love her, but it looked too much like the kind of thing they do in movies, so I just smiled and signalled that we'd talk later. Kneller said she asked J something about how you get back to the world of the living, and J told her it was a waste of time and that he'd show everyone the way to a better world. And when they went outside, she told Kneller that this J guy was just a bullshit artist. The music was so loud, I could hardly even hear Kneller. He was laughing a little at Leehee and me. He said it was the first time he'd met people who were more naive than him. Me with my miracles, and her with her dreams.

'Instead of offing,' he shouted, 'you should've gone to California.' I saw him patting Freddie, which meant they'd made up. Joshua climbed onto the stage, wearing his long gown, and Desiree followed him, holding a kind of curvy knife, like in the Bible stories for children where Abraham is about to sacrifice Isaac. She handed the knife to Joshua and the music stopped with a bang.

'What the hell is that?' Kneller muttered beside me. 'The guy's dead already. What's he want now, to be double-dead?' People nearby turned around and told him to shut up. He didn't give a shit, but me, I didn't know where to put myself. Then he said he bet J would never go through with it, 'cause anyone who's offed once and knows how much it hurts to die won't try it a second time. And just when Kneller finished saying that, J took the knife and stuck it right in his heart.

chapter twenty-five

in which a white van arrives and everything comes undone

Strange, but even though everyone around the pool knew the whole time what was going to happen, it still took us all by surprise. First nobody said anything, and then people started mumbling. From where she was standing on the stage, Desiree shouted to everyone to stay calm because J would be back in his body any minute, but they went on mumbling. Meanwhile, I saw Kneller whispering to Freddie and then, like, talking into his lighter, and in seconds a white van pulled up and these two tall, thin guys in white overalls got out. One of them was holding a megaphone. Kneller ran toward them and started talking to them and waving his hands all over the place. I started pushing toward where the women were to look for Leehee, but I couldn't find her anywhere. The man with the megaphone asked everyone to disperse quietly. Onstage, Desiree was sitting next to J's body and crying. I saw she was trying to get to the knife, but the other guy in overalls got to it first. He took it, then he lifted J's body over his shoulder and motioned Kneller to take Desiree to the car. Again, the man with the megaphone asked the crowd to disperse. Some of them started to move, but lots of others froze. I could see Leehee now, next to the man with the megaphone. She saw me too and tried to work her way closer to me, but the driver, who was also in overalls and kept talking into some kind of radio, called her over. Leehee signalled that she was coming in a minute, and I headed toward the van, shoving people out of the way, but by the time I got close enough, Kneller, with Freddie under his arm, and the overalls with the megaphone all got in the van and drove away. I could see Leehee in the window, trying to shout something to me, but I couldn't hear what it was. That was the last time I saw her.

chapter twenty-six
and on that optimistic note

I waited there another few hours, because at first I thought the van was only going to let J and Desiree off somewhere and that Leehee would be right back. There were still a few people hanging around. Everyone was in a daze. Nobody could really work out what had happened. We all sat there in these deck chairs around the pool, not saying anything. Then people began to leave, one at a time, and finally when I saw I was the only one left, I headed toward Kneller's house.

By the time I got there it was evening. Uzi said Kneller had rushed into the house to grab a few things and told everyone they could stay as long as they liked. Then he took Uzi aside and asked him to take care of Freddie. He let Uzi in on the fact that he never really offed himself and that all this time he was really an undercover angel, but that now with this whole Messiah King mess he'd blown his cover, and he'd probably go back to being just an ordinary angel. He told Uzi he didn't envy J, because bad as this place was, the place for the ones who do it a second time is a thousand times more grim, 'cause there aren't that many people there and everybody's totally fucked up. I asked Uzi if Kneller had said anything about Leehee. At first he said no, but later he told me that according to Kneller, Leehee had gone over to one of his people in the middle of everything and asked him to check her file, and even though it sounds crazy, it turns out that there really was some kind of mix-up and nobody knows what to do with her now, but that there's a good chance they'll take her away from here and bring her back to life. Uzi said he didn't want to tell me at first, 'cause I'd be upset, but that actually it's good news, because Leehee got what she wanted.

Uzi decided to stay at Kneller's place with his girlfriend, and I went back into town on my own. On the way, I even had the chance to perform a miracle, and that's when I understood what Kneller tried to tell me about how it doesn't really matter. I had this package that Uzi gave me to deliver to his parents, and they were really happy to see me. They wanted to know everything, especially about his girlfriend. Uzi's dad said Uzi sounded really happy on the phone, and that the whole family was going to visit him in a month. Meanwhile, they invited me to have Friday night dinners at their place, and in the middle of the week too, whenever I feel like it. The people at the Kamikaze were glad to see me too, and they put me right back on the shift.

I don't dream about her at night at all, but I think about her a lot. Uzi says that's just like me – to get stuck on girls I don't have any chance of being with. Maybe he's right, and I don't stand much of a chance. But on the other hand, she told me once that someone who was half dead was good enough for her, and when she got in that van she signalled to me that she'd be right back, so who knows. Just to be sure, every time I start a shift I do a little something – put my name tag on upside down, tie my apron the wrong way, anything, so if she ever does come in, she won't be sad.